Focus

The focus of this book is:

- to locate information on the page,
- to read for information.

Tuning In

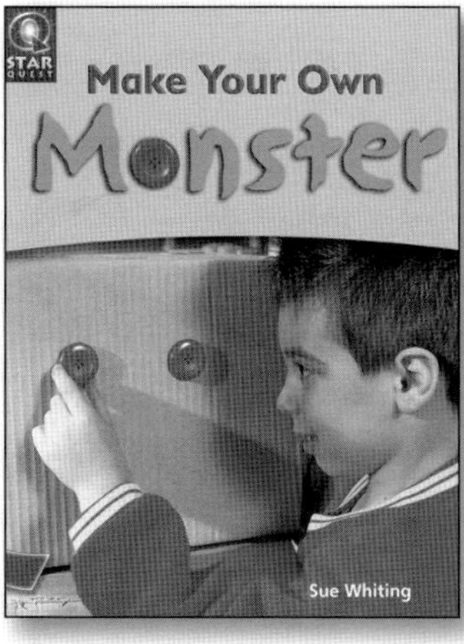

The front cover

Read the title and tell me what you think this book is about.

Speaking and Listening

You know how the writing would look on the page of a story book, how might this text be different?

The back cover

What does the blurb tell us about the book?

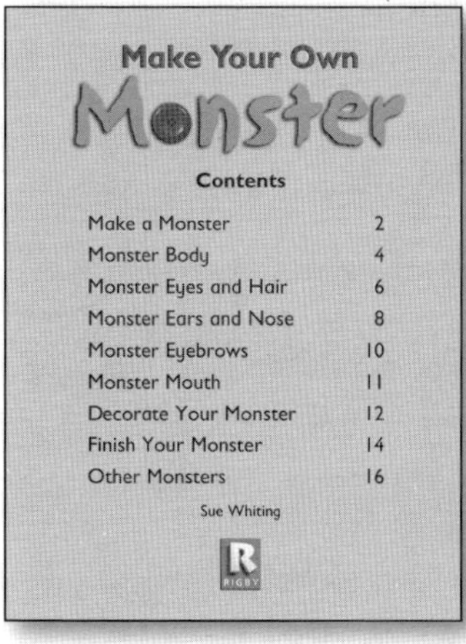
Make Your Own

Monster

Contents

Sue Whiting

RIGBY

Contents

What information does this page give us?

Speaking and Listening

Will we need to start at the beginning or can we choose any page to start?

Tuning In

What is the heading on this page?

What is the information on this page?

Speaking and Listening

Have you ever made a monster? What did you use to make it?

Make a Monster

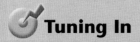

It's easy to make a monster.
This book tells you how.

Tools:

glue

paints

paint brushes

2

Prompt and Praise

Check that the children read the sub-heading 'Tools'.

Tuning In

Have you seen this before? (scouring pad) Where would you find it in the house? What do you think the boy will use it for?

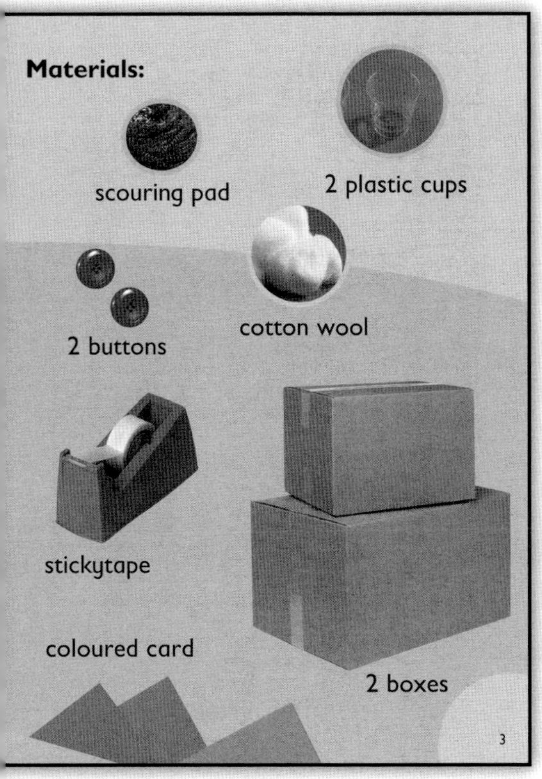

Prompt and Praise

Check that the children are reading all the text on the page.

Tuning In

What will you need to find first?

How will you make the box strong?

How will you use the small box?

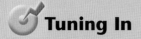

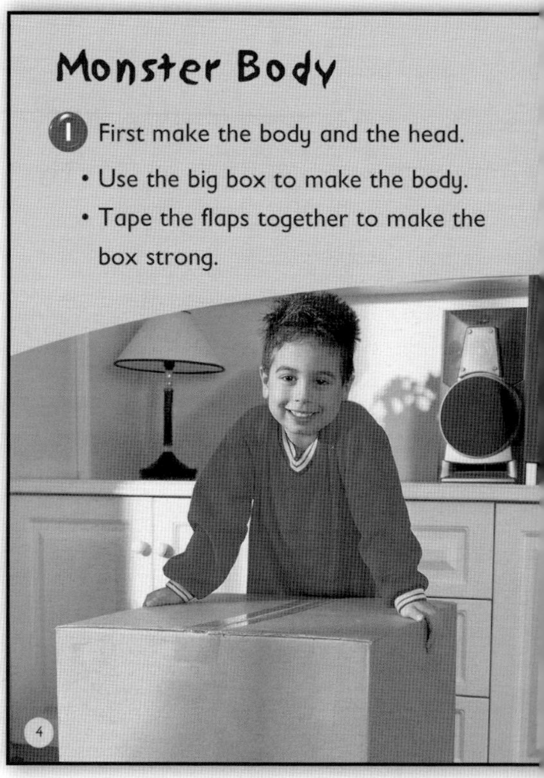

Monster Body

1. First make the body and the head.
   - Use the big box to make the body.
   - Tape the flaps together to make the box strong.

4

- Use the small box to make the head.
- Glue the small box to the top of the body.

Prompt and Praise

Check that the children are reading with expression.

Tuning In

Now what will you make?

What is the hair made from?

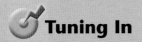

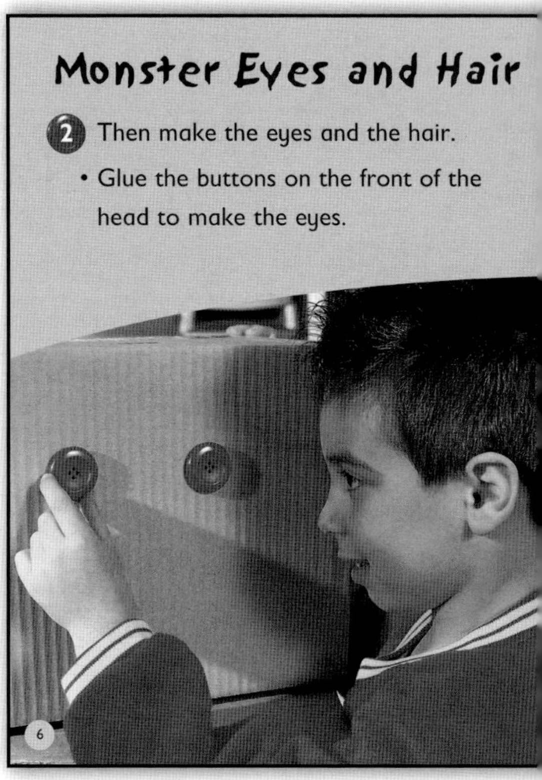

Monster Eyes and Hair

2 Then make the eyes and the hair.

- Glue the buttons on the front of the head to make the eyes.

6

- Glue the cotton wool onto the top of the head to make the hair.

7

Prompt and Praise

Check that the children have located all the text on the page.

Tuning In

Now what does the text tell you to make?

Where will you stick the cups?

What is the nose made from?

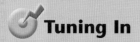

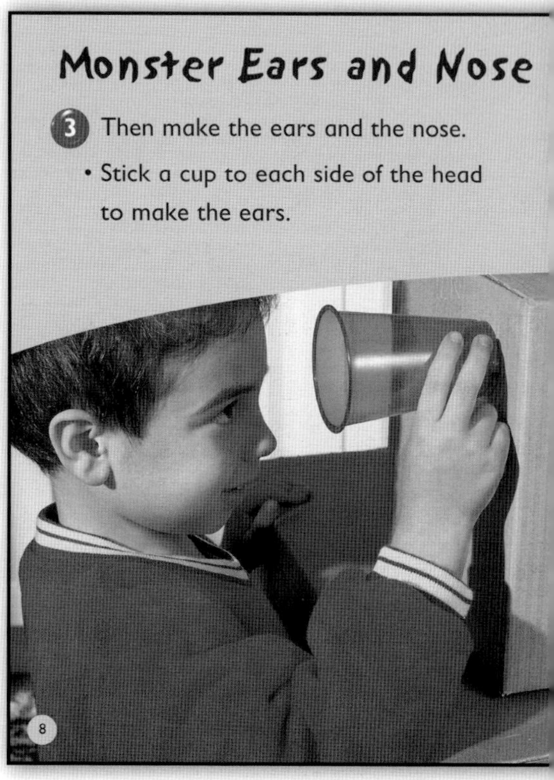

Monster Ears and Nose

3. Then make the ears and the nose.
   - Stick a cup to each side of the head to make the ears.

8

- Stick the scouring pad on the front of the head to make the nose.

9

Prompt and Praise

If children find 'stick' difficult prompt with a meaning clue, i.e. What is the glue for? Does that word look right for 'stick'?

Tuning In

Now what will the boy add to the face?

How has he made the eyebrows?

Monster Eyebrows

4 Now add the monster's eyebrows.

- Draw two triangles on some card.
- Cut them out and paint them.

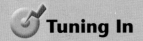

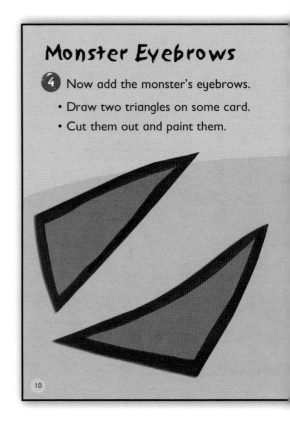

10

Tuning In

What is the mouth made from?

Monster Mouth

5 Then make the monster's mouth.

- Draw the mouth on some card.
- Cut it out and paint the teeth.

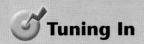

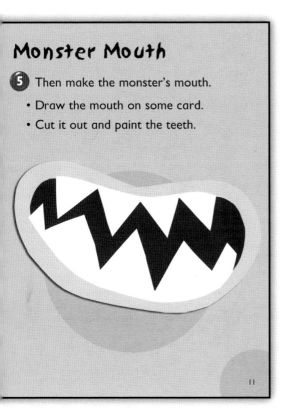

11

Prompt and Praise

If children find 'triangle' a problem, direct them to check the picture and divide the word into two.

Tuning In

What are the final instructions?

What will you need to make the hands and feet?

Decorate Your Monster

6 Finally, decorate the monster's body.

- Use the card and your paints to make two hands.

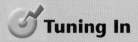

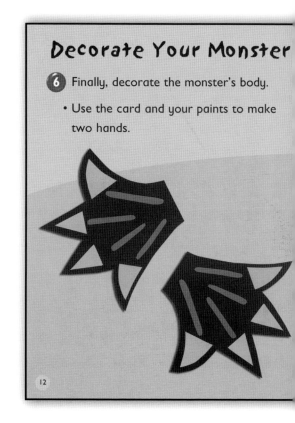

12

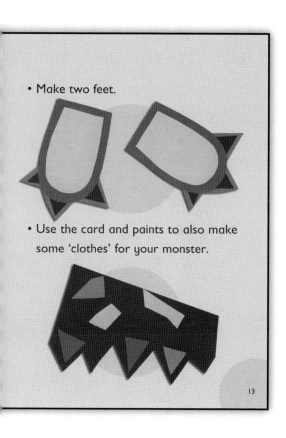

• Make two feet.

• Use the card and paints to also make some 'clothes' for your monster.

13

Prompt and Praise

If children find 'Finally' a problem, prompt with a meaning cue, i.e. What would we call the last instruction? Then ask if the words look right.

Tuning In

Where do you glue the hands, feet and clothes?

Finish Your Monster

- Glue the hands, feet and clothes to the front of the body.

Well done! You've made a monster.

14

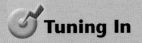

Prompt and Praise

Check that the children are reading all the text on the page.

Speaking and Listening

Do you think it's a good monster?

Tuning In

What other monsters could you make?

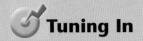

Other Monsters
What other monsters could you make?
16

Prompt and Praise

Check that the children are reading with expression.

Speaking and Listening

The boy made a monster. What type of things do you like making?